I Will Always Be Your Friend!

By Angela C. Santomero

Poses and layouts by Jason Fruchter

SIMON SPOTLIGHT

An imprint of Simon & Schuster Children's Publishing Division

New York London Toronto Sydney New Delhi

1230 Avenue of the Americas, New York, New York 10020

This Simon Spotlight edition August 2022

© 2022 The Fred Rogers Company.

For information about special discounts for bulk purchases, please contact Simon & Schuster

Special Sales at 1-866-506-1949 or business@simonandschuster.com.

Manufactured in China 0522 RKT

ISBN 978-1-6659-2078-0

ISBN 978-1-6659-2079-7 (ebook)

Hi, neighbor! It's a beautiful day in the Neighborhood of Make-Believe. There's so much to do and so much to see. And we can do it all together . . . because I love being your friend!

I love that we have great big imaginations!

We can play house: "I would like some tea, please!"

We can pretend to be dinosaurs: "ROOOAR!"

And we can even take off in a rocket ship: "Three, two, one, blastoff!"

I love being your friend.

I love that we can be silly together. We can make each other laugh and pretend today is "Backwards Day"!
I love being your friend.

I love that we are kind. We are big helpers,

we take turns,

and we always think about how someone else is feeling. I love being your friend.

I love that we always know how to cheer each other up. Whenever we are feeling blue, we sing:

 "It's okay to feel sad sometimes. Little by little, you'll feel better again!"

Singing with you always helps me feel better. I love being your friend.

I love that we stay by each other's sides when we're upset, like when it rains and we can't play outside. We remind each other that when we feel mad and want to roar, we can take deep breaths and count to four.

One . . . two . . . three . . . four. Counting helps calm us down. I love being your friend.

I love that we learn new things when we're together. We find shapes in the clouds,

look at twinkling fireflies,

and learn how to make things with clay.

We also visit the library, where we hear all kinds of stories about animals, rock crystals, Adventure Tigers, and more! I love being your friend.

I love that we try new foods too! Together we have tried foods like red bell peppers and veggie spaghetti.

We also eat banana bread and banana swirl! I love being your friend.

I love that we sometimes like the same things . . . but that we also like different things. You can do things in your own way, and I can do things in my own Daniel way! I love being your friend.

I love that you understand when I want to play alone sometimes. And when you don't want to play with me, I can find something else to do too. Even when we're playing apart, we are still friends!

Whether we're riding Trolley or visiting the Enchanted Garden, it doesn't matter what we do. I just want to be with you!